Dear Parents:

Congratulations! Your child is taking the first steps on an exciting journey. The destination? Independent reading!

STEP INTO READING® will help your child get there. The program offers five steps to reading success. Each step includes fun stories and colorful art or photographs. In addition to original fiction and books with favorite characters, there are Step into Reading Non-Fiction Readers, Phonics Readers and Boxed Sets, Sticker Readers, and Comic Readers—a complete literacy program with something to interest every child.

Learning to Read, Step by Step!

Ready to Read Preschool–Kindergarten
• short and easy words • rhyme and rhythm • picture clues
For children who know the alphabet and are eager to begin reading.

Reading with Help Preschool–Grade 1
• basic vocabulary • short sentences • simple stories
For children who recognize familiar words and sound out new words with help.

Reading on Your Own Grades 1–3
• engaging characters • easy-to-follow plots • popular topics
For children who are ready to read on their own.

Reading Paragraphs Grades 2–3
• challenging vocabulary • short paragraphs • exciting stories
For newly independent readers who read simple sentences with confidence.

Ready for Chapters Grades 2–4
• chapters • longer paragraphs • full-color art
For children who want to take the plunge into chapter books but still like colorful pictures.

STEP INTO READING® is designed to give every child a successful reading experience. The grade levels are only guides; children will progress through the steps at their own speed, developing confidence in their reading.

Remember, a lifetime love of reading starts with a single step!

W9-AXG-553

In memory of an English Mummy,
with love from her American Girl —R.M.

Step into Reading, Random House, and the Random House colophon are registered trademarks of Penguin Random House LLC.

Visit us on the web!
StepIntoReading.com
rhcbooks.com

Educators and librarians, for a variety of teaching tools, visit us at RHTeachersLibrarians.com

ISBN 978-0-593-38187-8 (trade) — ISBN 978-0-593-38188-5 (lib. bdg.) — ISBN 978-0-593-38189-2 (ebook)

Printed in the United States of America
10 9 8 7 6 5 4 3 2 1

★An A★G Girl®
Samantha Helps a Friend

by Rebecca Mallary
illustrated by Emma Gillette

Random House 🏠 New York

In the year 1904,

Samantha Parkington lives in

a big house with her grandmother.

She likes to climb trees

and make new friends.

Samantha always tells the truth,

and she will do anything

to help a friend.

Samantha's grandmother,
whom she calls Grandmary, wants
Samantha to be a proper young
lady and practice her embroidery—
but Samantha prefers adventures.
She often scrapes her knees
and tears her stockings!

Grandmary doesn't always approve of Samantha's fun, but she still loves her very much.

One of Samantha's favorite
people is her uncle Gard.
Uncle Gard lives in New York City
and has an automobile
that Samantha loves to ride in.
He is the only person
who calls Samantha by
a special nickname: Sam.

Samantha has a neighbor
named Eddie Ryland.
He is always teasing her.
But one day he tells her
something interesting.
There is a new girl next door!

The new girl is Nellie O'Malley,

and she works for Eddie's family.

When Samantha meets Nellie,

she shares a cookie with her

and they become friends.

Nellie has two little sisters, Jenny
and Bridget. Nellie and her sisters
have never been to school
because they had to work.
Now they will get to go
for the first time!

Samantha is excited as she walks
them to their first day of school.
Nellie is nervous, but Samantha
tells her it will be okay.

When Samantha comes to pick up
Nellie and her sisters after
school, everything is not okay!
Nellie is sad. She is crying
because the other children teased
her for being behind in school.
Nellie is in second grade, but
others her age are in third grade.

Samantha is sorry

to see her friend so upset,

but she has an idea of how to help!

Samantha sets up a schoolroom
in her house just for Nellie.
She will help Nellie
with reading, writing, and math
so that Nellie can move
to the third grade!

Nellie is happy when she sees
the room with a chalkboard,
books, and beans for counting.
Samantha is glad that Nellie
feels better.

Samantha goes to a school
called Miss Crampton's Academy.
At school, Samantha finds out
that there will be a speech
competition.

Every girl will give a speech
about progress in America.
Two winning girls will get to go
to a bigger competition!

Samantha is not sure what to say
about progress in America.
She decides to ask Grandmary,
Uncle Gard, and the butler,
Mr. Hawkins, about inventions.

Grandmary says the telephone
is the best sign of progress.
Uncle Gard chooses automobiles.
Mr. Hawkins thinks that factories
show America's progress.

Samantha goes to school
with a girl named Edith.
Edith teases Samantha for playing
with a poor girl like Nellie.
Samantha likes Nellie and
doesn't care what Edith says.

The girls give their speeches.
Samantha says that factories
show America's progress because
they make things quickly and
cheaply. She is chosen to go to
the big competition. So is Edith.

Samantha is excited to practice
her speech for Nellie! But
Nellie does not like the speech.
Samantha's feelings are hurt.

She asks Nellie why
she did not like it.
Nellie says it's because
Samantha's speech isn't true.

Nellie used to work in a factory.
She tells Samantha that factories
are dangerous for the children
who work in them.
They have to work all day long
and cannot go to school.
Sometimes they get hurt.

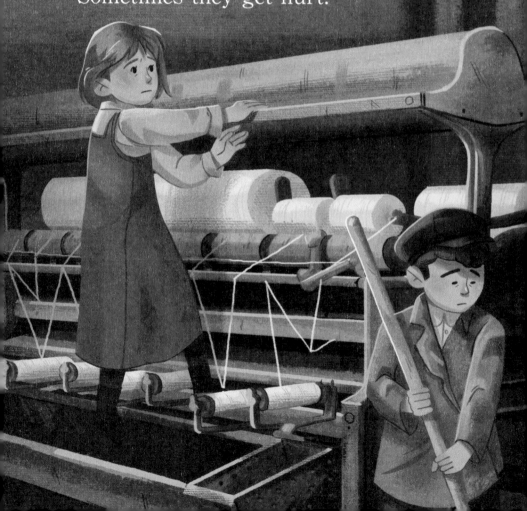

Samantha is surprised.

She did not know what factories

were really like. She wants

her speech to be honest.

At the competition,

Samantha changes her speech.

She talks about what factories

are really like.

She says that to have

real progress in America,

all children need to be safe.

Everyone is shocked, even
Grandmary. But Nellie looks happy.
Then Grandmary claps. Others do,
too. Samantha wins the contest!
She is proud she told the truth.

After the competition, Nellie
has some wonderful news.
Thanks to Samantha's help, she
is moving up to the third grade!
Samantha knew that Nellie
could do it!

Nellie tells Samantha that
there is just one problem:
in her new class, she sits
next to Eddie Ryland!

Samantha promises Nellie
they will keep working hard
so that Nellie can move up
to the front of the class!